YF Van
Van, Sandi.
Listen up

3/21

AR

POINTS_____

BOOK LEVEL_____

TEST #_____

**Sandi Van**

An imprint of Enslow Publishing

WEST **44** BOOKS™

Please visit our website, www.west44books.com.
For a free color catalog of all our high-quality books,
call toll free 1-800-542-2595 or fax 1-877-542-2596.

Cataloging-in-Publication Data

Names: Van, Sandi.
Title: Listen Up / Sandi Van.
Description: New York : West 44, 2021. | Series: West 44 verse
Identifiers: ISBN 9781538385265 (pbk.) | ISBN 978538385289
  (library bound) | ISBN 9781538385272 (ebook)
Subjects: LCSH: Children's poetry, American. | Children's poetry,
  English. | English poetry.
Classification: LCC PS586.3 L578 2021 | DDC 811'.60809282--dc23

First Edition

Published in 2021 by
Enslow Publishing LLC
101 West 23rd Street, Suite #240
New York, NY 10011

Editor: Caitie McAneney
Designer: Seth Hughes

Photo Credits: Cover (phone) FotoBob/Shutterstock.com.

Printed in the United States of America

CPSIA compliance information: Batch #CW20W44: For further information contact
Enslow Publishing LLC, New York, New York at 1-800-542-2595.

*This book is dedicated to all the students who have passed through my life and shaped my heart. Never let adversity keep you from your dreams.*

# Time

*Listen up, people.*

*Open your ears.*

*It's time.*

*Time for you to*
*STOP*
*giving in*
*to the system.*

*Time for you to*
*STOP*
*doing what you're*
*told.*

*Time for you to*
*STAND UP.*

*Be the force*
*that drives*
*change.*

*Be the one*
*who screams:*


*ENOUGH!*

# Courage

I stop the video.

The real world
waits for me.

Me:
       broken
       lost
       frozen

But first,
before
I let
the fear
creep
into me
like snakes,

I upload the video.

Add a clickbait title.

Post.

# The Real World

The one with teachers
and tests,
with parents
and an older sister
who does everything better.

In the Real World,
I am just Lucas.

When I hit record,
though,
I become
the Other Me.

The me who is not afraid
to say how I feel.

The me who is not afraid
to tell the truth.

# Family

My parents run
a real estate company.

Dad is the friendly one.

His face smiles
on the billboard
like his life
depends on it.

Mom is the smart one.

She balances the books,
the calendar,
the house,
like an acrobat in a circus.

They wanted us to follow
in the family footsteps,

but my sister Nell started college.
Pre-med.

And me?

Well, someday I'll be a star.

If I don't crash and burn
through the atmosphere
of high school.

# At School

It goes something like this:

I walk the halls.

Silent.

The sound of my own swallows
like a thunderstorm
in my ears.

Can anyone else hear that?

I want to talk.

Want to say,

*Hey man,*
*great job in the game last night.*

*Can you pass me a pen?*

*Did you see the latest upgrade?*

*How's the pizza today?*
*Carboard grease, as always?*

But it's like my brain
and my tongue
are in a constant battle.

They argue over what to say
and end up saying
nothing.

Or worse,
something dumb.

They fight
like a TV couple.

Only no one laughs.

Or maybe they do.
They laugh at me.

Laugh at me
standing there
like a fool.

My face hot.
My feet stuck to the ground.

My brain going
on and on
about something.

And then they walk away.

I've learned
it's better
to be quiet
than to
risk words.

# Pay Attention

Listen.
You can hear the sounds.

Voices
telling stories.

Listen.
You can hear the truth.

# Marnie

I see her
every day at school.

Our student council president.

Confident.
She seems
sure of herself,

but people aren't always
what they seem.

Sweet on the surface.
Sour underneath.

Hand in hand
with the same guy
since freshman year.
The most popular guy in school.

Greg Gale.

Smiles on their faces,
but not in their eyes.

Fear.
Doubt.
Mistrust.

I see the way he
squeezes
her hand
tighter
when they
walk by
other guys.

The way she checks in
every morning.

The way he talks about her
in the locker room.

The way she eyes him
up and down.

Makes sure his clothes
are just right.

Control.

On the surface,
they are happy.

They are the gods
of this school.

But there's always
more to the story.

# Stories

I watch
and listen.

Take it all in.

I watch Marnie.

The effort she makes
to stay popular.

To make sure everyone
follows her lead.

I want to know
if she ever feels
lonely
like me.

I watch groups
in the lunchroom.

Together
but alone.

Eyes focused on screens.
Thumbs sliding past life.

They instantly
dismiss
or accept
someone else's
breakable heart.

I want to know
why we worry
so much about
what other people
think but never worry
what other people
feel?

Every day I wonder:

Why can't we
treat each other better?

Why can't we
see past the
surface?

Why can't we
just *be*
human?

# Find a Way

When I walk
through the halls,
I want to scream.

Scream at it all.

But I can't.

Extreme social anxiety,
they say.

But my favorite teacher,
Miss Stone,
always says,
Find a way.

*Find a way to*
*be heard.*

# How It All Began

I got a laptop
for my birthday
last year.

Sixteen.

Mom thought it would
help me interact
more.

*You never touch your phone,*
she'd said.
*I'm worried about you,*
she'd said.
*Get an account on one of those sites,*
she'd said.

Make some friends.

Instead, I downloaded
software to
change my voice.
I found cool pictures
to create a background.

Instead,

I made videos.

# Is Anyone Listening?

The only trouble
with the videos I make:

They
have
zero
views.

# Until

lunch one day.

When Devin Maleny screams,

*HEY! HEY! CHECK THIS OUT!*

# The Ants Go Marching

His voice echoes
across the room.
It scrapes my ears.

The sound of chair legs
d r a g g e d
against the cafeteria floor.

All at once,
everyone rushes to see
Devin's phone.
Like ants that found a piece of candy
on the sidewalk.

Push.
      Shove.
*Let me see!*
      *Here it is.*
*What the—*
      *Who is that?*

Who is that?

I listen to the voice.

Disguised.

Mine.

# My Corner

I eat lunch
every day
in the corner.

The lonely kid.
Ignored by everyone.

      Peanut butter sandwich.
      Almond milk.
      An apple.

Mom stopped packing my lunch
in middle school.

But I find comfort in the foods
she used to choose.

I stare at the bite in my sandwich
and wish to be invisible.

They won't know it's me.
They can't know it's me.
I hope they don't know it's me.


Don't I?

# At First

there's laughter.
*Is this for real?*

And then—

quiet.

*Woah, dude.*
*Who is he talking about?*

*Is that us?*
*Is that here?*
*Is he for real?*

Knightsbridge High School.

It's in the title:

The Truth About the King of Knightsbridge

It's in my username:

The Lone Knight.

# The Lone Knight

Clever, right?

Because I'm all alone.

But I just want a chance
to save the day.

# The Students of
## Knightsbridge High School

gather around tables,
faces in their phones.

Click.
Click.

I pull mine from my pocket.

Watch
in amazement
as my subscribers
skyrocket.

I look at the video with
the most views.
Zero yesterday,
more than 30 today.

It's the one
where I called out Greg Gale
for talking about
Marnie's body
in the locker room.

So that's the video
that's made me famous.

I posted it last week.

Disgusted by the way
the other guys
talk about girls.

Like they are something
to possess.

A prize taken from a shelf
at the fair.

I don't want a girlfriend.
Or a boyfriend.

Which sometimes feels like
one more thing
that makes me different.

But the fact that everyone thinks
Greg and Marnie are so perfect
just really bothered me.

So I brought them back
down to Earth.

# What Happens Next:

I panic.

My heart pounds.

I reach up to my scalp.

Pull at the hairs near the back of my neck.

A habit that became a "condition"
when the school nurse noticed
the bald spot.

Pull my hand away.

Clench fists.

Try to become
invisible.


Wait.


I already am.

# After Lunch

I board the bus
for the Hyde County Occupational School.
HCOS for short.

Mom wanted me to go
somewhere
where I would "feel success."

So here I am.

Autobody and Collision Repair.

At first,
I thought it was dumb.

It's not like
I love cars or anything.

But taking something broken
and making it look brand new
is pretty cool.

HCOS is the bright spot
in my day.

Where I can work
on cars in peace.

Most days, anyway.

Today the bus buzzes
with talk of the
mysterious vlogger.

*Who is he?*
*He must be a student at Knightsbridge.*
*But who would do that?*

I stick my headphones in.

Call up a song on my phone.

Drown out the drones.

# It Doesn't Get Any Better

At HCOS,
students from Knightsbridge
tell students from the other schools
about the Lone Knight.

I haven't checked my phone
since lunchtime.

I'm too nervous.

# Here's the Thing:

I want people
to listen.

I want them to hear
what I have to say.

I want to
Stand Up,
Speak Out,
Make a
Difference.

But the reality
of who I am
versus
who I want to be—

I think
      it's a         gap
          too big      to cross.

# Fitting In

The other thing is:
I want to fit in.

Even though
the people around me aren't
the sort of people
who

understand.

Understand
what it's like
to feel stuck
inside my head.

Where words
bang around.

Demand to be free.

The people around me aren't
the sort of people
who

care.

Care about
the state of the world
the way I do.

A world that should be
full of kindness,

but instead

is full of cruelty.

# Example

There are other kids
at HCOS
who arrive
on a different bus.

Who have trouble talking
or can't get around the school
without help.

Who go to
a different class:
Life Skills.

And even though
we're all here
because we
need more than
books in a classroom,

I hear things.
In the hallway.

Unkind words.

Laughter.

We are all so desperate
to fit in,
sometimes we don't notice
who we're leaving out.

# Silent Partner

I try to ignore the gossip.
Focus on my work.

Today I'm partnered with Alise Garg.
She's from a different school.

I've noticed her before.
Sitting alone
like me.

We work in silence
for a while.

Awkward air
fills the space
between us.

# News Travels Fast

Classmates whisper.

*Did you hear?* I ask her
quietly.

*About, um. The kid who called out
that guy Greg from my school?*

I swallow.
Pick up a sander.
Try to pretend
I don't care about the answer.

       *Yeah, I heard,* Alise says.

I look at her.

Her eyes focus straight ahead.

I need to say something.
Anything.

I nod,
my head loose and
out of control.

My hands damp.

Alise says,
       *What a pig.*
       *I hope she dumps him.*
       *And quick.*

I smile at Alise
and say, *Yeah.*

Because that is a normal reaction.
I think.

# Off the Grid Girl

We work.

I watch Alise.

Study her.

She pushes the same black curl
away from her face
over and over.

I need to find out more.

*What did you think of it?* I ask.
Thankful my voice
didn't crack.

   *Of what?*

*The, um,
the video?
Did you watch
the whole thing?*

Am I wrong to think
she actually
wanted to talk to me?

   *Oh, that?*
She shakes her head.

*I didn't actually see it.*
*I'm an off-the-grid girl.*

*No phone.*
*No laptop.*

*Drives my parents crazy sometimes.*
*When they can't find me.*

*I tell them,*
*maybe I don't want to be found.*

She pulls the hood
of her sweatshirt
up over her head
and tightens the strings.

The curl pokes out
like an angry spring.

*Maybe*
*I like to stay*
*hidden.*

# A Friend at Last?

This girl is weird.

But also totally
my speed.

*I get that,* I say.

*The being hidden part.*
*And the phone part too.*

My eyes travel the room.
Phones aren't allowed during class.

And I know the minute
we're dismissed,
everyone will pull theirs out
for the latest updates.

*People are such drones.*

I think the words in my head
and then they exit my mouth.

Great.
Now she'll think
I'm a jerk.

Instead she says,
*Totally.*

Then looks at me,
pulls her hood down.
Her eyes move back and forth.

*What were we talking about?*

# Confused

I laugh.

Because I think she's kidding.
Trying to be funny.

She doesn't laugh with me.
Instead she asks,
>   *Did you just tell me a joke or something?*

What is wrong with this girl?
Is she high?

*Sorry, no*, I say.
My face feels hot.

>   *Okay, well, there's not much time left
>   in class*, she says.
>   *Let's work on this fender.*

# That Night

I open my laptop.

Log in.

I've gone from zero subscribers
to 50.

From single-digit views
to hundreds.

I'm afraid to read the comments.
So I don't.

At least not for now.

Instead I fire up the voice changer.

Slip on my headphones.

Position the mic.

Record audio.

# Another Way

*Do you want to know what's crazy?*

I say.

The voice is mine
and also not.

*We all look out for*
*number one.*

*What's in it for*
*ME?*

*But do you*
*ever*
*stop*
*to think*
*about what*
*other people*
*feel?*

*How the way*
*you behave*
*affects others?*

*Look around.*

*You have a choice.*

*Instead of trying to get people*
*to see things*

*YOUR WAY,*

*take a step closer.*

*Be a bit*
*kinder.*

# All Alone
## Among Friends

I talk about what I see
in the hallways.

About what I hear
in the lunchroom.

I talk about the
fallen faces
of rejection.

People need to see
what happens
when we look up
from our phones
and realize

we're

all

alone.

# School

Someplace where I

Can't escape the

Hallways full

Of laughter,

Of judgment, of

Loneliness.

# Changes

I used to like school.

When it was
colorful art projects
hanging in the hallway.

Story time
in the library.

When no one noticed
who left
the classroom
for extra
help.

In middle school,
people noticed
differences.

In middle school,
we sorted ourselves
into groups.

Who was good at what.

> Who had trouble
> with everything.

# Miss Stone

I've had Miss Stone since freshman year
in instructional support class.

ISC.

The class for kiddos
who need
a little extra help learning.

That's what she calls us.

Kiddos.

As in, *You kiddos ready to rock today?*

A question always met with
groans.

She's my ISC teacher again
this year.

*Hey there, my hardworking kiddos!*
she said on the first day
of eleventh grade.

*Glad to have you back.*

The thing about Miss Stone
that I like?

She never makes us feel dumb
or stupid
or less than.

She celebrates our strengths
instead of making us feel bad
when we don't understand something.

She tells us to share our dreams.

To imagine in our minds
where we want to be
and then make it happen.

# My Secret

When I was little,
a motivational speaker
came to my school.

He taught us about how to persevere,
to keep going when things got hard.

After, at home,
I lined up my stuffed animals
like an audience.

I used my hairbrush
like a microphone.

I told them stories.

Sang them songs.

Made them believe
in me.

Made them believe
in what I had to say.

# The Future

I try to imagine the future
in my mind.

Mom and Dad want me
to sell houses,

like they do.

But the future is not
my face on a sign
in someone's front lawn.

No way.

I want to stand
in front of a crowd
the way I stood
in front of my stuffed animals.

I want to stand
in front of a crowd
and inspire them.

I have a lot to say.

The trouble is,
I can't even stand up
in front of ISC.

# Not My Idea of Fun

Freshman year,
we had to write
autobiographies—
the story of our lives so far.

My English teacher that year,
Mr. Curtis,
thought it would be fun
to share them
out loud.

Fun.

I had to wear a hat that week
to hide the bald patch.

Miss Stone tried everything
to get me up front.

But I
couldn't
do
it.

# Hidden Behind the Mic

Mr. Curtis said
I could record myself instead.

Miss Stone let me use
the microphone headset
that students sometimes use
to write essays.

She played my project on a day
I wasn't in school.

So I didn't have to face
the laughter of my classmates.

She said everyone loved it.

# I Used to Think She Was Lying

But people watch
my videos.

They listen to
my words.

Maybe, just maybe,
people *do* want to hear
what I have to say.

# The Problem

My English teacher this year
is not as kind
and understanding
as Mr. Curtis.

Part of our English grade
this quarter
is an oral report.

Everyone must present
their report
out loud.

In front of
the entire class.

No excuses.
No exceptions.

Everyone.

Including me.

The kid voted
"Most likely to die of fright"
in our eighth-grade yearbook.

# I Don't Want to Talk About

what
happened
in
eighth
grade.

# Anger

*You know what makes me mad?*
I ask into the microphone.

Wondering who will listen.
Wondering what they'll think.

*What makes me mad*
*is people who are so afraid*
*of their own faults,*
*they spend their time*
*making fun of*
*everyone else.*

*Instead of lifting each other up,*
*we only lift ourselves.*

>  *"Look at me!*
>  *Look what I did!*

>  *Look at all the ways*
>  *my life is*
>  *better*
>  *than*
>  *yours."*

*You want to know*
*what I think?*

*I think we're all afraid*
*of being left behind.*

*Left out.*

*We don't take the time*
*to look around*
*and see what someone*
*next to us*
*needs.*

*A hug? Someone to listen?*
*Words that lift them up?*

*I challenge you, listeners.*
*Challenge you to open your eyes.*

*Look around.*

*Listen.*

*Find someone*
*who's been ignored.*

*Someone who needs a friend.*

*I challenge you to be good.*

I'm happy with the latest video.
No more silly gossip.

Now that people are listening,
I need to do something important.

# But

the comments start
before I have time
to close the screen.

The first few are nice.
Smiley faces and thumbs up.

    *You said it!*

And then:

    *shut up loser!!*

    *we want the T*

    *none of this feel-good crud*

    *get a life*

The hatred builds.

Like termites
eating away
at my heart.

I close the screen.

Close my eyes.

But the words continue.

I can see them—
hear them.

They won't go away.

Why did I think the internet would be
any different
from the real world?

# Rules

I have to play the game.
Do what they want me to do.
Say what they want me to say.
Be who they want me to be.

I like
the *r u s h*
the views give me.
I've had all I can take
of being
ignored.

I want the views.
I want the likes.
I want the comments.

Does that make me
a drone,
too?

# How to Gather Material

The next day I watch—
listen—
search for the thing
that will make me
famous.

Greg and Marnie are always
Hot News.

But Greg Gale is on guard now.

His eyes dart back and forth
around the room
as he tries to figure out
my identity.

The identity
of the Lone Knight.

The one who told the school—
who told the world—
what a creep he is.

Something we all knew
but no one would talk about.

The way he guards Marnie
from other guys
but then brags about
her body
when she's not around.

She's still with him.

I watch
and wonder.

Listen.

Her friends slam lockers shut,
and whisper behind hands.

There is more
to this story.

I can feel it.

I study Pria,
Marnie's best friend
and teammate.

Her right-hand girl
on student council.

They are the stars of
our varsity field hockey team.

Their faces make the local paper
every week

under **Athletes to Watch**.

So I watch.

# Selling Out

I record a video about how
student-athletes
get away
with more
than the rest of us.

Excused from assignments.
Dismissed from class.
Treated like gods.

Don't get me wrong.

They deserve to be celebrated
for their accomplishments.

But shouldn't we also celebrate
the most generous students
or the nicest ones?

The kid who stays after school
to sort through trash
for recyclables.

Or the one who holds the door
for the person behind her.

I think we should celebrate
the guy in the lunch line
who bought ice cream sandwiches
for everyone
when he finally passed a test
in chemistry.

Thoughts
that used to be my best videos
now seem too boring
for my ever-growing
audience.

I start over.

Instead of lifting up
the unsung heroes,
I gossip about
who dumped who.

And how they each cried silently
into their lockers until the bell rang.

The hits come
like I knew they would.

My heart beats hard
with the rush of attention.

I've never felt so alive.


I've never felt so ashamed.

# Family Night

Thursday night
is family night.

Dad and Mom have the night off
from work.

Nell comes home to do laundry
and raid the pantry.

She goes to college nearby
but decided to dorm.

It's been quiet at home without her.

She is gone, but not.

Her name is sprinkled into
every conversation
like salt.

# Tonight

she tells us all about
her organic chem class—
whatever that means.

And how everyone wants
to be her lab partner.

Mom and Dad smile at her.

Smiles I never see
when she's not here.

Their faces glow with pride.

*That's wonderful, hon,* Mom says.
*Wonderful.*
*We're so proud*
*of you.*

Dad nods.
Nell smiles back.

I chew in jealous silence.

*And how's junior year, punk?*
my sister asks.

      *Fine.*
      *It's fine.*

*You make any friends yet?*

She tilts her head to the side.

Raises her eyebrows.

Like I'm some sort of freak show
she paid to watch.

>*Nell*, Dad says.
>*Be nice.*

*I am being nice.*
*I asked about his life.*

My breath rises and falls in my chest.

Rises and falls.

Deep, slow, calm,
the way Miss Stone taught us.

*When you come across something*
*you don't know*, Miss Stone says,
*something confusing—*
*don't panic.*

*Breathe deep.*

My family feels like
something I don't know.

Like I've been delivered
to the wrong address.

I want to tell them what's going on.

With the videos,
with Alise.

How I might have
made a friend
if I don't screw it up.

I want to ask them what's more important:
being true to yourself
or doing what you need to do
to fit in?

A question I used to think
was straightforward.
Easy.

But we sit around the table,
crunch on lettuce leaves, and
listen to Nell.

I say nothing.

Nothing
is
easy.

# When We Were Kids

things were more equal.
Mom and Dad hadn't learned yet
how my brain was wired.

# Brain Switch

For a while,
I got all the attention.

While they tried to figure out
why I knew so much about the things
around me
but struggled to read.

Why I worried all the time
about stupid things.

Like how much toothpaste
was left in the tube.

Or if the picture I drew
had the right shade of green.

My brain stopped on
the strangest things.

Grabbed hold
and wouldn't let go.

If I said them out loud,
Mom would tell me
to focus on my schoolwork
instead.

Like I could flip a switch
in my brain.

Flip.

Just like that.

# Sometimes

my attention to detail
comes in handy.

I've got an A
in Autobody Repair.

The teacher says
I have a future there.

I could work in a shop
after high school.

I heard him say the same thing
to Alise.

Maybe we can be a team.

# Silent Alise

She's never said anything more
about the videos.

We focus on our job
in silence.

I try to think of
something smart to say.

I stare at her hands.
They're covered in a
red-brown ink design.

*You, um.*
*You did a good job there,* I say.

She doesn't answer me.
Makes a strange sound with her mouth.

I swallow and try again.

*Your hands? They're cool.*

Still no response.

I try to focus on our work
while my mind races.

Tells me horrible things
like how I'll never be
the sort of person
who has friends.

How everything I say
is dumb.

How I'm a LOSER.

Finally, she speaks.

> *Oh, this? Sorry, yeah, thanks.*
> *I did them myself.*

She puts the tools down
and holds out her hands.
Admires them.

> *It's henna.*
> *I like to draw.*
> *It helps me remember things, sometimes.*
> *The patterns.*

*Cool,* I say to Alise.

To my brain, I say:
HA.
TAKE THAT.
NOW BE QUIET.

# A Crazy Idea

I stare at her hands
and have a crazy idea.

*Hey, Alise?*

My mouth feels like
autumn leaves.

The words fall
one by one
into the room.

*Can*
    *you*
        *draw*
            *something*
                *like*
                    *that*
                        *on*
                            *paper?*

*For*
    *me?*

She picks up her tools.

Looks at her hands again.

Repeats my words
in the same tone of voice.

*Draw something like that, on paper?*
*For you?*

Is she making fun of me?

My fingers reach
for the back of my neck.

The voice in my head
is about to speak up again.

But then
Alise smiles.
     *Sure.*

# Around and Around

My heart is pounding
like I just took a big risk.
Stupid, maybe.

But I'm glad I asked.
I love the way the patterns
swirl around.
Like my thoughts.

# Step It Up

When I started
to make videos,
I knew my face
would never be on screen.

So I found stock photos
and loaded them into the video.

Cheesy zoom effects.
The occasional color burst.

Now
that I have
an audience,

I need to step up
my game.

# After Class

*You sure you're okay with this?*
I ask. *It's no big deal if—*

> *If what?* Alise looks at her hands.
> *The drawings?*

She pulls out her notebook
and begins a design.

> *Anything special?* she asks.

*No. Just draw.*
*Whatever.*
*You like.*

My words burst out
too loud,
too fast.

Alise doesn't seem to care.
She smiles.
> *Okay,* she says.

> *Thanks for being my partner.*
> *The last guy, he couldn't handle me.*

I swallow.

Couldn't handle her?
The look on my face
must tell her
I'm confused.

*Guess I drive people crazy sometimes.*
*When they have to repeat themselves,*
*ya know?*
*I don't listen too well.*

*Don't worry,* I say.
*I can't talk to people*
*too well.*

She laughs.
Pushes the curl
away from her face.

*Guess we make a good pair then, eh?*

# At Home

I scan Alise's pictures on
Mom's printer.
Mess with the colors a little.
Upload.

Wonder how I can give her credit
for the work.

Then I notice the letters of her name
swirled into the pattern.

A hidden signature.

I don't care what the last guy thought.

She's pretty cool.

# Is This What It Feels Like

to have a friend?

# The Feeling Doesn't Last

Back at school.
Back in my corner.
Back to being the kid
no one wants to
be near.

# It's Okay, Really

When you spend time
alone,

you spend time
learning
who
you want to be.

Because there's
no one
to tell you
otherwise.

# A Ship and Its Anchor

Have you ever noticed
what happens after
someone finds out
your secret?

When the tough
outside layer
of yourself
peels away?

I used to think Greg was just a jerk.

But maybe he's afraid.

Afraid of losing the anchor
that keeps him
from drifting away.

When I look closer,
I see the fear.

When I look closer,
I see the truth.

Shoulders slumped.

Shadows beneath the eyes.

Weak from the pressure
of being who he is.

Being who we've decided
he needs to be.

# Poetry

Today in English
we had to write a list poem—
which is when you take an idea
and list all the things that connect
that idea.

The topic: FEAR.

We had to brainstorm everything
that makes us afraid.

I didn't really get
how a list
could be a poem.

Someone in the class
asked what they should do
if they aren't afraid of anything.

The class laughed.

*We're all afraid of something,*
our teacher said.
*Snakes? Heights? Clowns?*

The class laughed again.

*If you can't think of anything,*
*make up an imaginary list.*

My classmate nodded,
satisfied with the answer.

I put my pencil tip on the paper
and thought,

What if I'm afraid
of everything?

# Fear

of snakes
of heights
of clowns

of tight spaces
of loud noises
of crowded rooms

of bees
of mice
of hurricanes

of people

of talking

of everything

# Fear Takes Many Forms

I feel better
when I see Alise
at HCOS.

We talk about cars.
I tell her about
the fear poem.

*What are you afraid of?* I ask.

   *Cars,* she says.

I think maybe she wants
to change the subject.

Maybe she wants to keep talking
about which paint color
matches the car we're working on
or how we're going to fix
the dented tire rim.

I ask again
in a different way.
Miss Stone says
sometimes that helps.

*What scares you?*

Alise looks me in the eyes.
   *Cars. Cars scare me.*

I tilt my head to the side.
*You aren't making sense.*

Which probably sounds mean.
But really.

We spend every afternoon fixing them.

> *I know,* she says.
> *But when I was younger,*
> *my mom and I*
> *got into a car accident.*
>
> *She broke her wrist.*
> *And I broke*
> *my brain.*

*What?*

> *The force of the*
> *crash.*
>
> *It broke*
> *my brain.*

# Broken

I stare at Alise.

She does not look
broken
at all.

Then I realize
why she
repeats things.

Why she sometimes
forgets what we're
talking about.

*It's called
traumatic brain injury,*
she says.

*TBI.*

*Parts of my brain
are totally fine.*

*But my memory ...
sometimes it doesn't work all that well.*

*I had to go to therapy
to relearn some stuff.*

    *Oh.*

That's all I can think of
to say.

She sighs deeply.
Keeps talking.

*So yeah, I'm afraid of cars.*
*But I figure—*
*if I work on them every day,*
*I'll overcome my fear.*

The thought of being
face to face
with my fears every day?

No way.

# Reasons

Sometimes
people get anxious
because of a certain
thing that happened.

You might be nervous
around bees
if one stung you
as a kid.

Me? I've always
had trouble
around people.

But life
has a way
of making it
worse.

# Eighth Grade Graduation

Our music class
was chosen to perform
at eighth grade graduation.

On the day she handed out parts,
the teacher came up to me and said,
*Lucas. I know you're shy,*
*so I'll give you just one line.*
*Okay?*

It wasn't okay.
But I couldn't tell her no.

My cheeks burned
as I nodded up and down.

I didn't know then
what I know now:

Social anxiety
is not the same
as shyness.

On the day of the show,
I hid in the bathroom.

Dad found me.
>       *It's only one line!*
>       *Just do your best!*
>       *It'll all be over soon!*

His voice like a game show host.

I went back to the gym.

I remember the lights.
A row of blinding suns.

I remember my body.
Stiff with fear.

Unable to move.
Unable to speak.

I remember the whisper in my ear.
Soft at first—
growing to a chant
that follows me like
a ghost
every day of my life.

Loser
Lucas.

# Loser Lucas

Like a thief
determined to steal
your cash,

the name followed me.

*Loser Lucas*

It followed me to high school—
in the hallways
and the classrooms.

*Loser Lucas*

Sometimes spoken out loud.
Sometimes in the eyes of
people passing by.

*Loser Lucas*

And when they grew tired
of the name,

it echoed in my head.

*LOSER.*

*LUCAS.*

# Practice Makes Perfect

I think about Alise's strategy.

Practice it by answering
a question
in chemistry class.
Tongue swollen.
Hands damp.

*An accelerant, like a car's*
*accelerator,*
*makes things go*
*faster,* I explain.

And no one laughs.

# The Next Step

Alise says I need to talk
to other people.

She lets me practice
with her.

What to say.

How to keep my mind
from stopping
my lips.

She says to go to school
and find someone
to talk to.

Anyone.

*You can do it, Lucas,* she says.

It feels strange
to have someone
believe
in me.

# Target Practice

I see Marnie
by her locker
after school.

I start to panic.

She is not the ideal
practice partner.

But Alise said
to pick
the first
available
target.

And maybe this will help me
get over the past.

I wait around the corner.

Watching.

Gathering courage.

But what I see
makes me change
my mind.

# What Happens

Marnie slams her locker shut.

The noise makes me jump.

I practice words in my head:
>    *Heading to your field hockey game?*
>    *Good luck.*
>    *You'll do great.*

Start to walk toward her.

She shifts to the locker
next to hers.

Her head twists left and right.
Left and right.

She doesn't see me.
I'm invisible.

Fingers spin the locker dial.

Lift.

Squeak.

Wait.

I duck behind the corner.
Something in my gut tells me
this is big.

Bigger than the need
to overcome my fears.

I pull out my phone.
Press record.

Marnie reaches into her bag.
Pulls on a pair of rubber gloves.

And something else—
something green.

Rubs it all over the inside
of Pria's gym bag:
    clothes
    shoes
    goggles

Her head twists again,
like an owl
watching for prey.

What is she doing?

What am I doing?

I stop the video.

Slip the phone back
into my pocket.

Silent.

Watch Marnie sling both bags
over her shoulder.

Close the locker.

Walk away.

# The Next Day

The next day I find out.

The next day everyone talks about
what happened
at the field hockey game.

The game the recruiters
came to—the Big One.

How Pria's eyes were swollen shut.

How bumps and blisters
appeared on her skin.

How anyone she'd touched that day—
a hug, an arm around the shoulder—
started to scratch too.

How Coach came over.

*Poison ivy*, she announced.
*Were you girls running in the woods?*
*What did you touch?*

They shook their heads.
        *No, Coach, no*, they said.
Even Marnie.
        *No, Coach, no*, she said.

But I know.
I know what really happened.

# What I Should Do

Go to the principal,
the coach,
Miss Stone.

Anyone.

Tell them what I saw.
Show them what I saw.

Anything.

# Why?

Everyone is human.
Everyone makes mistakes.

But why did Marnie hurt
someone she seemed to love?

# On Purpose

I try to let the Marnie thing go.
Really.

I want to believe she wouldn't
hurt her best friend
on purpose.

But my brain keeps circling
in an endless loop.

The events of the day
playing over and over.

The memory of her
standing at the lockers.

Touching Pria's stuff
right before she
got really sick.

Pria doesn't come back to school
for a week.

When she does,
her face is red and raw.
No makeup,
cheeks puffy,
arms covered in long sleeves.

Everyone crowds around her.
A chorus of:
>
> *Are you okay?*
> *We're so happy you're back!*
> *What a terrible accident.*

Followed by whispers when she walks away:
>
> *Did you see her face?*
> *That could scar!*
> *How could she be so stupid?*

Everyone assumes
it was something
Pria did.

Something
Pria touched.

Everyone assumes
it was an accident.

It WAS something she touched.

But I know
it WASN'T an accident.

# Responsibility

That night,
I make a decision.

The Lone Knight
has a responsibility.

To his fans.
To the world.
To Pria.

I tell the camera what I saw.
Exactly what I saw.

Pria didn't cause the rash
that spread around the team
to almost everyone.

Did anyone notice who didn't get sick?

Who knew to stay away that day?

Who played her best?

Who wowed the college recruiter?

# Perfect

*We all think*
*our student council president*
*has it all.*

*So why did she sneak*
*into her teammate's locker*
*and plant poison ivy?*

# Mistake?

The words leave my mouth.
My throat feels like it has been
scraped by broken glass.

# Actions Have Consequences

Marnie doesn't come to school
the next day.

Or the next.

I know
things
are
about
to
get
serious.

# Too Late to Turn Back

I start to worry.
Worry I've done
the wrong thing.

But it's too late
to turn back now.

To take back words
already
in the world.

# Something Missing

Everyone at school
is on edge.

Their queen bee
escaped the hive.

And now they fly around,
confused. On edge.
Not sure
where to go,
what to say,
who to be.

I never realized
how much a school
depends on
those they
choose to lead.

A country without
a president,

a pack without
the alpha,

becomes a place
of chaos.

# People Talk

and I listen,
the way I always do.

Whispered words about
the Lone Knight,
about Marnie,
her parents,
her reputation.

The school sits firmly
on her side.

I watch Pria,
once second in command,
now in the spotlight
for all the wrong reasons.

People spread rumors
they claimed to be the truth.

Pria had gotten sick
and blamed Marnie.

*Didn't you know?*

*That was the day the recruiters
came to their field hockey game.*

*The day they watched
with their clipboards
and their checklists.*

*The day they decided*
*who from Knightsbridge High School*
*was in—and who was out.*

# Sabotage

[sab-oh!-taj] v. 1. To interfere with, disrupt. 2. To damage someone's chances of getting what they want. past tense -ed (When Marnie spread poison ivy on Pria's bag, she *sabotaged* her teammate's chances of getting a field hockey scholarship.)

# Puzzle Pieces

The pieces fit together.
Like the puzzles Nell and I did
when we were kids.

She wanted to start
with the edge pieces
and work her way in.

*That's the way you do a puzzle,*
she'd say.

But I ignored her.

Instead I examined the patterns
on each piece.

Studied the way they
fit together.

I did the puzzle
from the inside
out.

# Motive

I sit in my room
and examine the pieces
of the Marnie puzzle.

It all makes sense.

*She needs to have it all.*

I used to think she stayed with Greg
because she was afraid of being alone.

I used to feel bad for her
when Greg was a jerk.

But she is the one who makes sure
he looks and acts exactly
how she wants him to look and act.

She is the one who keeps their image
shiny and picture-perfect.

I get that feeling again—
like there's more to the story.

Maybe she controls him like
she controls the rest of the school.

Maybe she'd do anything
to have it all.

*She needs to have it all.*

# Hideaway

Mom and Dad
want to know
what I do up in my room
all night.

*Studying, I hope,*
Mom says.

She has not given up
on the idea of me
joining the family business.

*You're a smart boy*
*and could do anything,*
*if you put your mind to it.*

She refuses to accept
that my mind already
decided
it doesn't like to be
put
anywhere.

# Family Bonding

After dinner, Dad says,
*Let's watch a movie together.*

So we sit
on the couch.
Four minus one.

Nell's absence is felt
in my mother's sighs.

It's felt in my muscles,
relaxed—
not missing
the pressure
of comparison.

Dad turns the TV on.

*Oh, let's watch the news
for a minute,* he says.

*They're doing a story
on that new development
on the west side of town.*

We watch.

Everything is fine.

Normal.

Except for the feeling
of terror
that washes over
my whole body.

# Everything Is Fine

Everything is fine.
Everything is fine.
Everything is fine.

Until it's not.

# Everything Is NOT FINE

*After the break, we'll learn the truth*
*about what happened last week*
*at Knightsbridge High School.*

Mom says, *Lucas,*
*stop pulling on your hair.*

Dad squeezes my leg.
            *You okay, buddy?*

No.

I am not okay.


After the break
After the break
After the break

Marnie is on TV.

# Two Sides to Every Story

Marnie is on TV.
Marnie's parents are on TV.

They went to the local station
to report
their side of the story.

How Marnie had nothing to do
with the field hockey team's
mysterious rash.

She is innocent.

- ✓ straight-A student
- ✓ captain of the field hockey team
- ✓ president of the student council
- ✓ Ivy League-college bound

*But you know who isn't innocent?*
her father asks the television audience.

I sit on my hands.

My heart
thumps in my throat.

Marnie's mother looks at the camera.
She stares right at me.

Her words stab me in the gut.

*The Lone Knight.*

*Whoever they are,*
*they need to apologize*
*for the lies*
*they've spread*
*about our daughter.*

*The lies they've spread*
*about the students*
*at Knightsbridge High School.*

*They need to be*
*caught.*

*They need to be*
*stopped.*

# Lucas?

Mom asks.

*Do you know anything about this*
*Lone Knight character?*

The sides of my throat
glue shut.
I shake my head.

    *Such a shame,*
Dad says.

    *She seems like such a nice young lady.*

    *What a terrible thing*
    *to happen.*

Why is everyone
on her side?

# Stupid or Brave?

I think for a moment
about what I've done.

Think for a moment
of turning myself in.

But then I realize.

Now is not the time to
be silent.

Now is the time
to fight back.

# Justice

After the movie,
I go to my room.

Think.

What would Miss Stone do?
What would Alise do?

They would face the fear.
They would do what's right.

I will face the fear.
I will do what's right.

*You may have heard my name*
*on the news tonight,*
I say into the mic.

*You may have heard them say*
*I told lies.*

*But I told*
*the truth.*

*Marnie hurt her friend.*
*She hurt the team.*

*She wanted the coach*
*to focus on her.*

*It isn't right.*

*Pria shouldn't be punished.*
*She deserves justice.*

# Rat

I close the laptop.
Afraid of what will
happen next.

Will they figure out
it's me?

Will I forever be known
as the kid who
ratted out
the student council
president?

# Two Sides

Everyone in school has
a theory.

Everyone in school has
chosen sides.

More and more
people
turn
against
Marnie.

I see her face fall
when she is rejected.

Even after all she's done,
it hurts to see her hurting.

I should have seen it coming,
but it's still hard to watch.

I wanted to tell the truth.
Not destroy someone's life.

# Worried

Alise isn't in class.

Which is weird because
she's never been absent
before.

During break,
I wish I could pull out my phone
to call her
and make sure she's okay.

But I don't have her number.
I remember
her rule about
no phone.

# Really Worried

Something is definitely wrong.

Alise is absent again.

What if people saw
her drawings and think she's
the Lone Knight?

I ask the shop teacher
for her home number.

Tell him I need to ask her
something
about the repairs.

It takes a lot of breaths
in and out
to work up the courage
to dial her number.

Her mom answers.

Says Alise hasn't been feeling well,
and would I like to come over?

# Comfort Zone

Calling Alise on the phone
was hard enough.

How the heck do I
gather the courage
to go to her house?

Miss Stone's voice in my head
says, *If you ever want to grow,
you need to push out of
your comfort zone.*

There's another voice in my head
that says,
*You're a loser.*
*She's not your friend.*

I try to ignore it.

Alise IS my friend.

And I need to talk
to her.

# Mistake

A woman
answers
the door
and it
feels
like
a million
spiders
are dancing
in my gut
and I
can't tell
if I'm just
nervous
or if
something
is terribly
wrong.

# Spiders

*Hello,*
the woman says.

She wears a purple dress and pants—
a *salwar kameez,* Alise told me once—
and has the same dark
brown eyes as her daughter.

It takes me a minute
to find words.

Finally, I say,
> *My name is Lucas.*
> *I'm uh—*
> *I'm a friend—*

*Oh yes, please come in.*

Everything seems fine.

Except I can't get
the spiders
in my gut
to quiet down.

# Unfriendly Greetings

Alise stands at the top of the stairs.
*Oh, it's you,* she says.

Not the hello
I expected.

We sit in the family room.

Alise's mom brings us creamy tea
in tiny white cups,
and small yellow cookies.

      *Your house is nice,* I say.

It smells amazing,
and the tea is spicy and sweet.
They call it chai.

We drink the tea and eat the cookies.
No one talks.

Sip.

Chew.

Sip.

Chew.

      *Is everything, um, okay?*

I ask between bites.

Alise looks up.

Pushes the curl away from her face.

*No.*
*No, it's not.*
*It's not okay, Lucas.*

*Or should I say,*
*"the Lone Knight"?*

# Identity Revealed

My heart stops.

How does she know it's me?

I stare at her hands,
at the faded ink.

Duh.
The drawings.

> *I, uh, I thought you didn't—*
I can't finish the sentence.

Alise's eyes burn a hole
right through me.

*I looked up the video,*
she says,
*after I saw it on the news.*

*You never said*
*that's why you wanted my drawings.*

*Are there videos about me?*
*About what I told you?*

*People don't know.*
*It's private.*
*Lucas, this stuff is private.*

Her words are fast
and sharp.

She's right.
I feel awful.

I set out to do something good,
but it turned into something terrible.

I try to explain to Alise
that when I started,
I wanted the world to see
we're all human.

That I never meant
to hurt anyone.

But the words sit in my throat
like heavy stones.

And now,
instead of being a hero,

I am a monster.

# Dismissed

*Lucas,*
she says,
her voice clearer
than I've ever heard it.

*You need to go.*

# Remorse

I ride my bike
away from her house.

The wind in my face is
cold and angry

like Alise's eyes.

How do I make things right with her?

How do I tell the truth
without hurting people?

# Back to the Beginning

That night,
when I try to sign into my account,
a message appears.

The account has been reported.

I delete the account in fear.

Everything is gone.

I have no voice.

I am back
to being
alone.

# It Doesn't End There

The next day in school,
we're called to the office
one
by
one.

It wasn't enough
to shut down
the Lone Knight.

Marnie's parents want
to find out who
RUINED
their daughter's life.

I try to stay calm.

But the what-ifs spin through
my head like one of those fidget spinners
they banned in school.

Meant for kids like me
who need to focus
on one thing.

Meant to quiet
a noisy brain
and fingers
that won't stop
moving.
But too many kids
played with them.

Until the thing
meant to help me focus
became
a distraction.

Now I wish I had one
to keep my fingers
from doing
what they shouldn't.

To keep my mind
from going
where it shouldn't.

To keep my mouth
from saying
what it shouldn't.

# My Turn

I make a decision.

One that would not
make my parents
or Miss Stone
proud.

I lie.

# It's Too Late

Rumor has it
Marnie's parents
are going to hire someone
to trace the videos.

To find out where
they were posted from
and who posted them.

I hear this in the hallway.

And I worry
it's only a matter of time
before they find me.

# Then Something Crazy Happens

I open my school email:

      club reminders
      sports schedule
      Spring Talent Show

The same boring emails
from student council.

Except.

There's one titled "Open for the Truth."

It's from Marnie.

# Open for the Truth

**Open for the Truth**

Dear Classmates,

I'm sorry for the investigation
that's hanging over all of us.
Distracting us from our lives.
Ruining our school year.

All because one person
had to call me out online.

To that person: I need to talk to you.
Explain what really happened.

My parents will find you
whether you like it or not.

Come to me,
or I'll
come for you.

Your President,
Marnie

# Decision

I blink.
Fingers freeze over the keyboard.

There is no easy way out of this.

I open a new tab.
Sign onto the email account I used
to start my channel.

Copy Marnie's email.
Type a response.

**Open for the Truth**

Marnie,

Meet me by the tennis courts before
morning bell.

The Lone Knight

# Regret

The second I hit send,
I wish I hadn't.

Regret rushes in
like a flood
and tries
to drown me.

# Now What?

What do I say to the girl
who thinks I ruined her life?

And what will she say to the boy
who knocked her from her throne?

I will be the one
she least expects.

# Or Maybe Not

After all,
she was the one
who called me out
at the eighth-grade celebration.

As we stood on stage,
and I prayed for the Earth
to swallow me whole.

She was the one
who kicked my shin
to try and defrost
my stiff body.

Even though nothing—
not her smile,
not a thousand suns—
could melt it.

When her quiet attempts
failed,
she spoke two words
that echo in my ears
every day.

Two words that started a chant.

*Loser Lucas.*

So yeah,
I guess a part of me
is happy she went down.

That I knocked over
her portrait of perfection.

That I made her crime
public instead of handling it
quietly.

Maybe 10%.

The other 90% feels
like
nothing
but
garbage.

# Wait, Watch, Listen

I sit hidden
on the grassy hill
behind the tennis courts
for a full hour.

Waiting.

Watching.

Listening.

The things I do best.

# Confront the Enemy

Marnie arrives.

I watch her through
the windows of
her mother's SUV.

Her body stiff and scared.
I've never seen her
like this before.

She opens the door,
and I hear the words
that flow
between Marnie
and her mom.

*Marnie,*
her mother barks,

*you need to make things right again.*
*You need to make them pay.*

And Marnie's voice, weak and quiet:
*I know, Mom.*

My palms sweat.

I pull at my hair with one hand.

Wrap the other arm
around my legs.

This was a bad idea.
A terrible idea.

The whole thing.
All of it.

# Unexpected

Marnie steps out of the car.
Slams the door.

Her mom rolls down the window.

*Listen to me, young lady,*
she says.

Her voice like flames.

*You need to convince them*
*to take it all back.*

*Admit they made*
*a mistake.*

Marnie walks away
from the car.

But I know she hears her
mother's harsh words.

*Don't you dare come back home*
*unless you do.*

*Do you hear me?*

Marnie keeps walking.
Her steps on the pavement
are loud and quick.

*Do you HEAR me?*

The SUV drives out of the lot,
tires screeching.

Marnie stops.

Holds her hands
in front of her face.

Sweeps them into her hair
and pulls.

Pulls her hair
like she's trying to
yank it out
by the roots.

# Mistaken Identity

I stand up.

Walk toward the girl
in the parking lot.

The one I thought
I'd understood.

The one everyone
at school looks up to.

Worships.
Adores.

And I realize
that there is more
to a story
than good guys
and bad guys.

Sometimes
the line between
what's right
and what's wrong
is blurred.

# Deal with the Devil

She stops when she sees me.

*You?* she says.

Her voice carries the
same flame
as her mother's.

I sit, frozen.

She towers over me,
blocking the sun.

*You're that jerk who ruined
the eighth-grade show.*

No words.
Only fear.

*Look. Let's make this simple.*

*Here's what happens next.
You admit to everyone at school
that you were wrong.*

*What's your name again?
Lenny?*

Lucas, my brain says.
Loser Lucas.

My mouth says nothing.

*Whatever.*
*Tell them you were wrong.*

*That I had nothing to do*
*with Pria's rash.*

She stands, hands on hips.

*Don't you know how to talk?*

# Two Sides of the Same Coin

Her words bite.

But I can't stop thinking about her
hands pulling on her hair.

Or her eyes, deep brown
and full of pain.

I stand up.

*I do know how to talk,*
*actually.*

*My name is Lucas.*
*I am the Lone Knight.*
*And you are lying.*

# Checkmate

We face each other
like knights in battle.

*Prove it*, she says.
Her voice shakes
ever so slightly.

I reach into my pocket.

Pull out my phone.

Cue up the video of her
at Pria's locker.

Press play.

# Apology

Marnie's face loses
all color.

Now she is the one
who cannot speak.

*Look*, I say.

*I don't want to hurt you.*

*I never meant for a war.*

*I just wanted to do the right thing.*
*Justice for Pria.*

*But I let the fame*
*go to my head.*

*I put the problem*
*out in public.*

*To give myself a voice,*
*to keep people hooked.*

*For that, I am sorry.*

I slip the phone
back into my pocket.

# Humans in Battle

Time tilts the ground beneath us.
Each waiting for the other
to take the next step.

*Please*, Marnie whispers.
*I need that scholarship.*
*My parents—*

Her hand reaches for her hair,
but she pulls it back.

Words spill out like blood
from an open wound.

*I tried to get the grades,*
*join all the clubs,*
*be the best.*

*But it's never enough.*

*They said I had to get the field hockey*
*scholarship or there wouldn't be*
*enough money for college.*

*And Pria,*
*she's better than me.*

*And I care about her,*
*I do.*

*I never meant for her to*
*get so sick.*

*I thought it would*
*distract her.*

*Thought she would make*
*mistakes.*

*And the coaches would notice*
*me instead.*

*Instead*
*I ruined her chances.*

*And I came here today*
*to ruin your life too.*

*I'm sorry, Lucas.*

# Now What?

The wind shifts.
Collects leaves from a nearby tree
and sends them to the ground.

I watch them fall
alone

and land together.

*We need to fix this,* I say.

Together.

# The Problem Is

I have no idea how
to work together.

# Trust Me

Marnie stares at me.
*What do we do?* she asks.

Waits for an answer.
Shoves her hands into her pockets.

I know that move.

The leaves fall one by one
in a graceful drop
to their death.

> *Let me think about it,* I say.
> *We'll figure this out.*
> *Trust me.*

I've never said those words to
anyone before.

People have said them to me:
>> doctors
>> parents
>> Nell (right before she does
>> something untrustworthy)

But I've never asked
someone to
trust
*me.*

# Loop

All day, I try to
come up with a solution.

My brain loops around ideas
like a model train at the toy store.

Finally, I know what to do.

# Step One

Fix things with Alise.

Thankfully
she's in class today.

But she still won't talk to me.

Today we're learning how
to estimate cost.

I feel confident.
I'm good at math.

Alise sits next to me
and scribbles on her paper.

*I keep forgetting to add the tax,*
she says.

To herself?
To me?

Her hair is braided
long and neat down her back.

The angry curl
threatens to pop out.

She pushes it away
and growls.

I swallow.
Breathe.

*Can I help?*

# Apology, Apology

We work on the problems together.

*Thanks*, she says at the end of class.

    *No problem.*

We walk side by side
toward the exit.

    *Alise*, I say,
    *I'm sorry about not telling you.*
    *About the videos.*

    *The truth is, I didn't think you'd find out.*
    *And I didn't want you to judge me.*
    *Or tell me it was dumb.*

Tell me *I* was dumb,
I think to myself.

*I'd never say that, Lucas.*
*You are a good person*
*with a big heart.*

I smile.

Repeat my apology, so she hears it again
and remembers.

She smiles back.

# Friendship Fixed

*Did they take them down?* Alise asks.
*The videos?*

*I did,* I say.

I tell her about Marnie.
About the scholarship.
The video I took on my phone.

How we were both wrong
and now we have to
make things right.

We stand on the sidewalk.
Wait for the buses
in the warm fall sun.

*Did I tell you about my accident?* she asks.

I nod.

*Then you know how I used
the fear and pain
to turn my life around?*

I nod.

*Our suffering is caused
by our own actions.*

*We choose how to react.*

I shrug my shoulders.
  *Huh?*

Alise closes her eyes.
Holds her palms out toward the sun.

*Lucas,* she says, her eyes still closed.
*Take what you fear.*
*Make it your strength.*

She opens her eyes.

*Part of my therapy,* she says.

*It's called a mantra.*
*A saying you repeat*
*when you're afraid.*

Alise reaches out and grabs my hands.
I try to pull away,
but she holds them tightly.

Buses screech into the lot.
Students push and shove past us.

*Are we okay?* she asks.
*I'm sorry I got mad.*

I take a deep breath and
squeeze her hands.
  *We're okay,* I say.
  *Thank you.*

# Mantra

Fear into strength.
Fear into strength.
Fear into strength.

# Best-Laid Plans

I sit down at my desk.
Pull out a notebook and pen.
Write what I plan to say.

Not what I plan to say
into a camera—
my face and voice disguised.

What I plan to say
to the school
onstage.

# How Do I Get There?

I know being able
to speak in front of people
isn't as simple
as flipping a switch
in my brain.

So I talk to Miss Stone.

Ask her if she can help me
overcome my fear
the way Alise is
overcoming hers.

Then I find the number
of the field hockey recruiter
and give it to Marnie.

She asks if they could visit
our school again.

The recruiter says no, she can't come out.
But the players are welcome to
send in a highlight video.

There is plenty of time
before they make any decisions
about the scholarship.

Plenty of time
for Marnie to make things
right.

# Step Two

I ask Marnie to schedule
a student body meeting.

She agrees.

Tells me she's stepping down
from student council,
but this will be
the last thing she does.

She says, *I'm sorry about eighth grade.*
*I didn't realize how much it hurt you.*

*I watched your other videos*
*before the account was deleted.*

*You have a lot of*
*interesting*
*things*
*to*
*say.*

# Miss Stone

helps me figure out
what I want to say

and how I WILL be able
to say it.

# The Road to Okay

I know Miss Stone
can't fix everything.

I ask my mom
to make an appointment
with a counselor.

Her name is Beth.

She says we can work together
to train my brain
to be okay
in difficult situations.

She doesn't think
my brain
is broken
or less than.

She doesn't think
I'm a loser.

She tells me I'm
      creative
      interesting
      kind.

The work we'll do
will give me the chance
to show the world
all those qualities.

# Fight or Flight

On the day of
the student body meeting,
my body puts up its usual fight.

Hands: cold and numb.
Mouth: dry and closed.

Miss Stone gave me something
to keep in my pocket
and click
instead of pulling my hair.

She said my brain
is strong enough
to win any battle.

I repeat my mantra
and take the stage.

The crowd buzzes
like killer bees
on the attack.

Marnie says my name.
Stands next to me.
Smiles.

I want to give up.
Sit down.

I want to run away.

Hide in the bathroom
the way I did in eighth grade.

But that is the old Lucas.

The new Lucas is able
to work through
his fears.

# Keep Going

*Classmates,* I say.
My voice is loud
in the microphone.

A few pockets
of laughter.

Followed by
*Shhh!*

*Classmates,* I say again.
*I have something to tell you.*

*It's not easy for me to stand here,*
*as many of you may know.*

More laughter.
Quieter this time.

*But I want to tell you*
*that I am sorry*
*for any hurt*
*I may have caused.*

Pause.
Breathe.

Fear into strength.
Fear into strength.
Fear into strength.

*For any hurt*
*I may have caused*
*as the Lone Knight.*

Words rumble through the crowd
like an oncoming storm.

My heart pounds faster and faster
until I worry
I may pass out.

Worry this will end
the same way it did
in eighth grade.

Marnie stands by my side.

This time, instead of whispering
words of cruelty,
she says,

>   *Keep going.*
>   *You got this, Lucas.*

I've got this.

*When I started the channel,*
*I was angry*
*about the way people*
*treated each other.*

*I've been angry*
*about the way people*
*treated me.*

*But instead of joy,*
*I brought pain.*

*I made decisions*
*and said things*
*without thinking.*

*We are all flawed.*
*And we are all good.*

*We need to celebrate*
*what we have in common*
*instead of looking for*
*what drives us apart.*

*We need to see the person*
*next to us and lift them up*
*instead of stepping on them*
*to get ahead.*

# Let's Practice

I say.

Sounds from the crowd.
Followed by shushing from the teachers.

I turn to Marnie.

*Marnie, you are a strong leader.*

A tear falls down her cheek.
Her lips mouth a thank you.

She takes the microphone from me.
My heart races.

Will she follow my lead
or go back to her old ways?

Marnie clears her throat.

*I am also sorry for the hurt I caused.*
*I did do what the Lone Knight said I did.*

Suddenly everyone is talking.
I see the fear in Marnie's eyes.
She speaks over the crowd:

*I know it doesn't fix what I did, but*
*I nominate Pria to take my place*
*as student council president.*

She turns to me.
*And Lucas, I never realized*
*how smart you really are.*

*And I'm sorry for not*
*giving you a chance before—*
*to share your ideas*
*with our school.*

*Thank you.*

I take the microphone back.
Wait for the chatter to die down.

*Your turn,* I say to everyone.

*Turn to your neighbor and tell them*
*something positive.*
*I like your shirt,*
*or you're good at math.*

It's quiet at first.

And then we hear the happy sound
Miss Stone likes to call
"creative buzz."

My heart pounds.
Not from being nervous,
but from being happy.

# Can Do

After being up
on stage,

the English report
doesn't seem so scary.

I'm still nervous,
but now I know
that I can do it.

# The Good Knights

Marnie, Alise, and I decide
to start a new video channel together.

Where we talk about the good things
we see at our schools.

Where instead of gossip,
we celebrate everyday kindness.

We call ourselves
the Good Knights.

# Better Than Okay

When you are
alone,

you spend time
learning
who
you want to be.

But when you are
with friends,

you spend time
learning
how
to be
human.

# WANT TO KEEP READING?

If you liked this book, check out another book
from West 44 Books:

### *CONTROL ROOM*
### BY RYAN WOLF

ISBN: 9781538385203

# HELIORAS WELCOMES YOU!

## An Introduction
## to the Present Moment

# GROWTH

When he switches on
the lights,
my eyelids
snap
down.
Block out
the sudden white.

I hold myself
        inside
the bright red
behind my lids.
Then blink
the room
into focus.

"How are you feeling,
Maggie?"
        Terrance asks
        with too much
        sweetness.
"Are you well?
I feel
just terrible
about bringing you here
last night.

This was only
        a misunderstanding."

I won't say
anything.
I'm a child
tossed
in time-out.

I won't give
adult answers
to a man who isn't
        my father.

Terrance leans in
to touch
my forehead.
His blond bangs
        hang
        over me.

"Your energy is low,"
        he says
        with his usual calm.
"But I don't judge you.
        Or think
        any less of you.

You don't think
        less of a seed
        because it isn't
                a tree.

I know
the love inside you
        will grow."

**CHECK OUT MORE BOOKS AT:**
www.west44books.com

An imprint of Enslow Publishing

# WEST 44 BOOKS™

# ABOUT *the* AUTHOR

Sandi Van is a writer, counselor, and former special education teacher from Buffalo, New York. She is the author of the young adult verse novel, *Second In Command*, and her poetry won recognition in the *Elmira Star-Gazette* and the PennWriters' In Other Words contest. Sandi draws inspiration from former students and admires those around her with the bravery to speak up for what they believe.